This book is for N

For information address Hyperion Books for Children,
114 Fifth Avenue, New York, New York 10011-5690.

First Edition
1 3 5 7 9 10 8 6 4 2
Printed in Singapore.

Library of Congress Cataloging-in-Publication Data
Raschka, Christopher.
Sluggy Slug / by Chris Raschka.—1st ed.
p. cm.— (Thingy things)
Summary: Sluggy slug will not go because he is sluggy.
ISBN 0-7868-0584-6 (trade)
[1. Slugs (Mollusks)—Fiction.] I. Title II. Series: Raschka,
Christopher. Thingy things.
PZ7.R1814S1   2000
[E]—dc21   99-39077

Visit www.hyperionchildrensbooks.com,
part of the GO Network

THINGY THINGS
Sluggy Slug

Chris Raschka

HYPERION BOOKS FOR CHILDREN
NEW YORK

Sluggy Slug won't go.

No, Sluggy Slug
will not go.

Sluggy Slug says no.

Sluggy Slug just won't go.

Will he go now?

No. Sluggy Slug won't go.

Sluggy Slug!

NO.
Sluggy Slug

simply won't go.